The Hagstone

By

Da

First published in 2001
by Anglia Young Books
Anglia Young Books is an imprint of
MILL PUBLISHING
PO Box 55
4 Balloo Avenue
Bangor
Co. Down BT19 7PJ

Illustrations by Robin Lawrie

British Library Cataloguing-in-Publication Data

A catalogue record for this book is available
from the British Library

ISBN 1 871173 61 2

Printed in Great Britain byAshford Colour Press,
Gosport, Hampshire

The Hagstone

Author's Note

In the Twenty-First Century we live in times when communication between people is quick and easy. We have friends in other countries, but we can talk to them by phone or on the internet. People have jobs which cause them to fly to the other ends of the earth. Man has been to the Moon and back.

But in the late Sixteenth Century when this story is set, life was different.

Travel was difficult and dangerous.

There were bad roads and maps were not good. Inns were dirty and flea-ridden, while the landlord was likely to be a spy for cruel robbers.

Ten miles was a long day's walk in those days, so many people never left the villages. There was no postal service, no telephone, no electronic machines. If one of the family went to work as a servant, they had only one day every year when they were allowed to pay a visit back to their home. That day was sometimes on a Sunday in Spring, and became known as Mothering Sunday, the day when the mother saw some of her children again.

But sometimes a town would have a yearly Fair, and there would be a holiday for that too. Fairs were great days for a town. Anyone who had anything to sell - food, cloth, hand-made wooden toys, ribbons, cheap jewelry - set up their stall and shouted their goods at the top of their voices. Farm animals were driven in and flocks of geese added their honking to the noise.

There were street entertainers too: jugglers amazed the crowds with their skill; fire-eaters swallowed yellow flames and spat them out again; acrobats and tumblers were everywhere. The crowds threw pennies to them.

Then there were the cheats and tricksters. Some sold pills and medicines that really cured nothing. Magic tricks made money for the trickster but never for the poor fair-goer.

Children born into a rich family lived comfortable, easy lives. They ate good food and dressed in good clothes. Boys went to schools where they learned Mathematics and Latin. Girls were taught at home and learned how to read, write and take charge of a household. Servants were there to see that life was good and free from trouble for everyone in the big house.

But poor children had very different lives. Their houses were small with low walls and thatched roofs. There was often just one room where everything took place. Sleeping and eating all went on in there. The cooking fire's smoke had no chimney to go up, but went out through a hole in the roof. Their food was basic and their lives were mostly nothing but work.

The poor family in this story talk of how life was better before their rights were changed. In the Middle Ages, people who lived in a village could all keep a pig and a cow, grazing them on the village common and in the forests. Wood for their building and for fires could be gathered from the forests, too. Crops were grown on strips of land in the village fields and there were few fences and hedges. But by the time this story took place, wealthy people had started to fence off the common lands and put sheep there. Sheep made a lot of money for the landowner, but meant that the poor people had nowhere to graze their cows. Then a lot of the woods were cut down so that the family pig had nowhere to find nuts and roots. Life became very hard. The man of the house now had to go and work for somebody else instead of being his own master. Women and girls had to spin the sheep's wool in the cottage to make more money. Food had to be bought instead of grown. Things were very different.

All this meant that many families now had very little to live on. Some of them went out begging, often disguising themselves as old, ill, crippled, blind and so on. Some men got together in bands and became robbers, attacking travellers on lonely pathways or picking pockets in the towns. Children were taught how to beg and steal. There was danger in taking any long journey.

So, in 1575, Queen Elizabeth

the First was reigning over a country where some people were getting very rich. Towns were getting bigger and trade with the rest of the world was increasing. But for the poor in England, life was a struggle and living was hard.

School was only for the lucky ones, so people believed in all kinds of things that today we laugh about. They thought that witches and evil spirits might be everywhere. Those who went to church - and most of the country people did - said their prayers and that helped them. But some carried lucky stones, charms, four-leaved clovers, rabbits' feet, anything that they thought would protect them from harm. One of these was known as the hagstone, and was just a stone with a hole through it, either made naturally or made by man. Some of these stones were hung over the bed to keep away illness, some at the doorway to scare witches and evil things away.

Some were huge with a hole so large that it could be crawled through: people with bad legs, stomach ache or broken arms might be passed through that hole in the belief that they would be cured. Some very small hagstones were hung round the neck. Why were they called hagstones? Because hag was another name for a witch.

Anyone wishing to read more about stones and the part they played in our country's history might like to read a book by Janet and Colin Bord, entitled 'The Secret Country'. Look on the beach next time you are at the seaside. You may find a hagstone among the flints, so that you can keep one in your desk, just like the writer of this story does. It is not likely to do anything more than just lie there, but it is good to feel that you will be doing something done by young people in this country hundreds and hundreds of years ago.

Chapter One

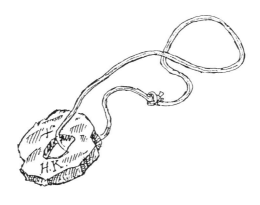

'Hark! Hark! the dogs do bark; beggars are
            coming to town,
Some in rags and some in tags and one in a
            velvet gown.
Some gave them white bread
And some gave them brown;
Some gave them a whipping and drove them
            out of town

The year was 1575 and the town was
waking up. Summer was nearly over but
it was going to be another hot day. It was
also going to be an exciting day, for it was

the day of the great Fair. Once a year the busy town was closed off. On this day no animals or carts could use the street. Stalls were set up to sell all kinds of food and goods and the people enjoyed a day with no work.

Well, not everybody had no work to do. Outside the house of Henry Kett, a rich wool merchant, a young man was standing. He was sucking his left thumb and muttering because he had just hit it with a hammer. This was Alan, apprentice to Master Kett.

'Windows!' grunted Alan. 'I hate these glass windows. Last Fair Day three of them got broken. So here I am, nailing wood over the glass.'

He picked up his hammer, held a board over the small window and hammered nails to hold it to the wall. 'Now his precious glass can't get smashed,' he said to himself.

Inside the house it was cool and dark. Tom Kett, only son of the family was not in a good temper. It was his tenth birthday and his father was not at home. 'He promised me a present,' Tom said to his mother. 'A hawk for hunting. Why has he forgotten?'

Mistress Kett frowned. 'Forgotten? He has not forgotten. He has had to go across the sea to the Low Countries, to Antwerp where the great wool merchants gather. You will get your hawk when he returns - that is if you stop moaning and do something useful. Go and help Alan make the windows safe. The fair starts today and the town will be full of strangers.'

'Are you sending me to go and help the servants?' Tom said. 'I don't do servants' work. Look, I am wearing my best blue velvet doublet and new leather shoes.'

For the rest of the morning Tom was in a really bad temper. He would not play with his smallest sister at hop-scotch in the yard. He would not help his middle sister weed her herb garden. He shouted at his oldest sister who wanted him to help her to write a letter. 'You go to school,' she said. 'Show me how to make my words look right.'

'Do it yourself,' said Tom grumpily. 'Boys go to school to learn Arithmetic and Latin, not to do letters for girls.'

To make things worse, the midday meal was not good. Susan the maid had left bones hidden in the fish and Tom got

one in his mouth. He spat it out on the floor. His mother scolded.

Then the apple pudding was spoilt because Susan had used salt instead of sugar. 'I'm sorry,' she wept when Tom's mother shouted at her. 'The windows are all boarded up, so I could not see properly. And it's Fair Day as well. I can think of nothing else. I should like to go.'

'Well, you can't,' said Tom. 'But I shall go.'

'No, Tom, you will not go,' his mother said. 'It is too dangerous, with all the beggars and thieves about. We have a Constable but he does nothing but ride around in his big hat, taking no notice of them.'

'I will take care,' said Tom. 'I promise.'

'I said no. Wait until your father gets home.'

'But he may be a week and the Fair will be over.'

His mother looked at him. 'Do you promise to stay out of trouble? If you speak to people at the Fair like you speak to our servants they won't like it.'

Tom said, 'I promise. I will take Alan

with me. He's big enough to keep trouble away.'

Mistress Kett said, 'Oh well, go on then. It is your birthday, after all.' She turned to Susan who was still looking miserable. 'And take this snivelling girl with you as well. She will do no work here with that going on in the street. Off you go.'

Outside, Alan had finished boarding up the windows, and now he was standing on a stool to hang something over the door. It was a round, flat stone, rather like a huge, thick coin. It had a hole through the middle, big enough for a man's thumb to go through. 'It's the hagstone,' Alan said. 'We must hang it up or bad luck will come to the house. Master says it keeps witches and bad spirits away. See, it has the sign of the cross scratched on it.'

'I know all that,' said Tom. 'But how could an old stone keep a house safe? Here, give it to me.' There was a leather band passing through the hole in the stone. Tom had watched his mother make the band out of deerskin. He put the leather round his neck, so that the hagstone hung on his chest. 'There,' he said. 'Let's see if it will keep evil spirits away from me.'

Alan said, 'I was told to hang that up again. Now I shall be in trouble. Give it back to me and I'll take my club instead. That will keep us safe.'

'You do as I say. When we come home, you can hang it again. Nobody will know.'

Susan said, 'Take care, Master Tom. That really is magic. Last month when I cut my finger on the big knife, that stone made it better. All I did was put my finger through the hole and the blood stopped. Well, not at once, but next day it had all dried up.'

All around them the noise was terrible and the street was full of people. 'Pooh! The smell!' said Tom, wrinkling his nose. At that moment a beggar with only one leg hobbled by. A ragged black cloak hung from his shoulders. His face, legs and arms were covered with bruises and sores and he had a patch over one eye. 'Spare a penny for an old soldier, just back from the wars,' he croaked.

Tom drew back and Alan aimed a kick at the beggar. 'Clear off,' he yelled, waving his club at him. 'I know your tricks.' He pulled at the beggar's cloak, and there was the man's other leg! It was tied up and hidden it under the cloak, to make people think he had lost it in a battle.

The beggar hobbled off, cursing. 'Take no notice of beggars like him,' Alan said. 'If you threw him in the town pond, all those sores would wash off. He's as fit as me and a lot richer.'

They walked on. Street singers were singing old songs. All round them traders were yelling about what they had to sell. In one place a crowd had gathered at a honey stall. They wanted honey to sweeten their food and beeswax to make their candles.

'What's going on over there?' asked Tom, pointing to a group of people near the church porch. Smoke was rising from a small fire. As they got close they saw a tall man, dressed in brilliant yellow and red clothes, waving a long wooden staff in the air. On a small table lay a black cooking pan.

'Listen to me, my friends,' the man
was saying. 'This is your lucky day. I am
the Great Saltimbanco, Marvellous Man

of Magic, and this staff and this cooking pan were given to me by the Grand Cham of China.'

The crowd gasped. Not many of them had heard of China but it sounded as if this man had travelled far and met amazing people.

'These are not ordinary things,' the man went on. 'I will show you. Come closer and watch.'

He lifted the iron pan and placed it on the fire. 'I'm hungry,' he said. 'But I have no food. What can I do?'

The crowd roared. 'Stay hungry, like the rest of us,' a man shouted. 'You won't get anything to eat from an empty pan.'

Saltimbanco narrowed his eyes and pointed a long finger at the man. 'Take care, my friend,' he said. 'The Great Saltimbanco has a way of dealing with people who mock him. Just watch.'

The pan was getting hot. Saltimbanco took his staff and began to stir inside the pan, muttering as he did so, 'Grand Cham, Grand Cham. The Great Saltimbanco needs food. Oh, Grand Cham, hear me.'

He stirred and smoke from the fire rose

into the still air. He made a pass with his hands over the fire and green sparks flew upwards. The crowd gasped and moved back a little.

'Watch!' said Saltimbanco. 'Watch and wait. It is about to happen.'

Chapter Two

The flames from the little fire licked round the pan. Everything had gone quiet. Saltimbanco went on stirring and muttering. Then Tom heard somebody whisper. 'What's that? It smells just like fried eggs!'

And as Tom and the rest pressed forward to see, there was no doubt. The pan was no longer empty. There in the bottom of it was a small pile of what looked like scrambled eggs, cooking in fat and giving off a very good smell.

'Magic!' the crowd murmured and

some looked afraid. An old woman made everyone jump by shrieking, 'Witchcraft! The man's a witch!' Tom felt a shiver run up his back. He reached up to touch the hagstone round his neck for luck.

But Saltimbanco shook his head. 'No witchcraft,' he said. 'Just very useful Chinese magic that I learned from the Grand Cham. At the same time that he gave me the earthquake pills.'

'Earthquake pills?' a man said. 'What are earthquake pills?'

'Oh, never mind about that. Here, just taste these eggs. Good?'

The man reached into the pan and grabbed a fistful of egg. He crammed it into his mouth. Black grease and yellow yolk ran down his beard. 'Good!' he said. 'Make more!'

Saltimbanco shook his head. 'No, the pan will only work once every day. And in any case I must go. I have to take my earthquake pills to the people in the next village. They have promised to pay me good money.'

Those at the front of the crowd were scraping the pan clean. 'No, don't go,' they said. 'Show us these earthquake pills. Why should the next village have them? We want some.'

Saltimbanco reached in a pocket and pulled out a small bottle. Inside they could some tiny white pills. 'These,' he said, 'are a sure way of keeping your houses and your children safe. Just swallow one of these pills and your house will never, ever be struck by lightning or shaken to bits by an earthquake.'

'Give us one,' shouted the crowd. 'We want one.' But Saltimbanco said, 'Well, I suppose I could spare a few. The other village said they would give me two pence for each pill. Just two pence and you and your children need never fear death by earthquake.'

While that was going on Tom had wandered round the back of Saltimbanco's table. The wooden staff was lying on the ground. The crowd were pushing round the magician offering money so Tom was alone. He bent down and picked up the staff. Then he saw how the egg trick worked. One end of the staff was hollow and there were traces of white fat all round it.

'So that's how he does it,' thought Tom. 'And he's going to take money off these poor people. I must stop him.'

He was right. People were giving Saltimbanco money. Tom heard a woman say, 'I will give you all the money I have for that pan.'

'How much have you got?' Saltimbanco said. Tom could stand it no longer. He picked up the staff. He opened his mouth to shout, 'Don't buy, it's all a trick,' but before he could say one word, a rough sack was pulled down over his head. His hands were forced behind his back and he felt himself being picked up and carried away.

Tom kicked and struggled. But it was no use. He was thrown down on his face and his hands and feet were tied. Then the sack was taken off his head.

They were in the churchyard. Four or five men stood looking down at him. He tried to give a yell, but one of the men bent down and stuffed a cloth into his open mouth. Tom kicked at the man but a fist came down and hit him in the mouth.

'Do that again and I'll throw you in the river,' the man said.

The gang's leader was short, fat and filthy. Dark, greasy hair straggled down over his face which bristled with a stubby beard. His clothes were thick and ragged. A long cloak hung from his shoulders.

Tom stared at him. He knew him. It was the beggar at the door, the man who had pretended to have only one leg. The fake sores had been washed off and the eye-patch had gone, but Tom was sure it was the same man.

The beggar grinned, showing black stumps of teeth. He twisted Tom's ear and breathed foul breath in his face. The man's hand was brown and filthy with broken nails. Tom saw with a shudder that the thumb was not there, just a ragged stump.

'Look at me, insect,' said the beggar. 'That's right. I am that poor man in the street who only wanted a penny. Your servant gave me a kick, but now I can get my own back.' He lifted his foot, but one of the other men grabbed his arm.

'Leave him, Stumper,' the man said. 'Just let's get his clobber and slit his throat. He's seen too much.'

'Yes, strip him,' said another. 'I fancy that velvet cap. I'd have his doublet as well but it's too small.' He turned to a third man. 'Here, Titch, you try it.'

The man he spoke to was small and hunch-backed. He undid Tom's hands and tore off his doublet. Then he pranced around with it over his shoulders. 'Bow down!' he cackled. 'I'm the King of the Beggars.'

The man called Stumper took Tom's belt and purse and his shoes were pulled from his feet, leaving him in just his under-shirt and hose. One of the men reached down to grab the under-shirt, but as he did so he saw the hagstone hanging round Tom's neck.

The man's face went pale. 'Here. Lay off, mates,' he said. 'Look at this. I've heard about these things. That's witches' stuff.' He made the sign of the cross and backed away.

Stumper looked. 'Pah. Nothing,' he said. 'I don't believe in all that stuff about witches. Let him keep it. See how much protection it gives him when you stick a knife in him.' He cackled with laughter. Then his face grew angry again. 'But he's seen too much. You, Black John, slit his windpipe. Dump his body in the churchyard and let's be done.'

The others were looking afraid. Tom started to sit up but Stumper hit him in

the face and knocked him back again. As
the boy lay there he kicked him in the
ribs. 'All right,' he yelled. 'Just get rid of
him. Take him and throw him in the
river. No, I tell you what, over there's the
donkey cart of that so-called wizard from
China. Chuck the little devil in it. Let
that mountebank try and explain how he
came to be there.'

He kicked Tom in the ribs again. 'You,
insect. If I hear that you have said one
word about who did this, I shall come in
the night and slit your throat from ear to
ear. Like this.' He raised his knife and
Tom felt a sharp prickling sensation near
his ear. Salty blood ran into his mouth.

'Get rid of him!' said Stumper. He
cuffed Tom's ears and two of the men
dragged the boy by his heels to where a
small donkey cart was tied to a tree. 'Put
him in there. That cheat will not find
him until he's miles away.'

The rough sack came down again
over Tom's head and he felt himself lifted
up and flying through the air. He landed
with a thud on boards at the bottom of
the cart. Splinters sliced into his bare

arms. Dirt and dust filled his mouth and nose. Then his head hit something very hard so that bright stars flashed in his eyes. Gagged and tied in a sack, Tom lay there, bruised and bleeding, crying with pain.

At last, after a long time, he heard a voice and the cart started to move. Tom's head bounced up and down on the floor and after a while everything went black and he fainted.

Chapter Three

In the Kett household there was panic. Alan and Susan had got back to the house and were trying to explain what had happened. Mistress Kett was screaming at them.

'There was this magic man,' Alan stammered. 'Everybody was watching him. Made eggs out of air, he did. Tell her, Susan.'

Susan was sobbing with fear. 'True, mistress. We were watching that and smelling the lovely smell of eggs cooking. Young master, he sort of left us.'

'Sort of left you?' screamed Mistress Kett slapping her round the head. 'You brainless, stupid, blind toad! How did he leave you? Where did he go?'

'I don't know, mistress.' Susan was really howling now. 'We looked everywhere. He just sort of vanished, like...like...like magic.' Her eyes grew wide. 'You don't think the man magicked him away?'

Mistress Kett slapped her again. 'Stupid girl! Stop that row and run for the Constable. Tell him to get a search started. Tell him my son is lost and must be found. And listen, you two nincompoops, if Tom is not found very quickly, you...you... I will have you both tied to the whipping post and beaten until you...until...Oh, don't stand there dithering. Go!'

Susan ran. 'And you,' said Mistress Kett to Alan. 'Go and ask if anybody has seen him. Your life will not be worth living if he is not found before my husband comes home.'

Alan ran into the street. Two men on stilts strutted past him, holding out their ragged hats for pennies. Across the road an old man was pushing a flaming iron rod into his mouth. He blew out a red squirt of flame and croaked. 'I eat fire. I eat fire. Penny to see me eat fire.'

The crowd was very thick now and Alan had to force his way. A woman caught at his coat as he hurried past. 'Sweet apples, young sir,' she said. 'Buy my sweet apples.'

But Alan had no time to waste. He made his way to the churchyard where he had last seen his young master. The Great Saltimbanco had gone and his place had been taken by three boys and a man who were tumblers. They stood on their heads, did cartwheels and climbed on each others' shoulders before tumbling down into a smooth somersault.

The crowd clapped. Alan said to a boy, 'Where is the man who made magic eggs?'

The boy shrugged. 'Gone,' he said. 'Sold all his pills and went off in his cart.'

'Did you see my young master? He wore a blue velvet hat and doublet.'

The boy shook his head. As he did so a man came up. 'No sign of that Saltim cheat,' he said. 'I gave him two pence for one of these pills, but now the Priest tells me they are just sugar and water. They will never keep earthquakes away. The rogue tricked us.' He looked at Alan. 'Who is this?'

The boy said, 'He was asking about the magic man.'

The man caught Alan by the scruff of the neck. 'Are you mixed up with that rogue?' he hissed. 'If you are... '

Alan struggled free. 'No. No. A young boy is missing, and if that Saltimbanco has gone, perhaps he has taken him. My master is a magistrate and my mistress is asking the Constable to start a hue-and-cry.'

The man said, 'Is that so? Then I will join in with it. I am a watchman. Go back to your mistress and tell her that the Watch will be called out. I want to settle with that trickster. I want my money back.'

Soon the street was buzzing with the news that the son of one of the richest men in town was missing. The Constable, in his tall hat, was gathering the Watch. 'There will be a reward!' he shouted. 'Any man who joins in this hue-and-cry will be rewarded. Mistress Kett has promised. Arm yourselves and meet by the church. Hurry.'

Mistress Kett watched them go. She looked up at the sky. It was beginning to get dark and it looked like rain. Where could her son have got to?

She turned to go in, but as she did so three men on horseback rode up. It was her husband and two of his servants, back from Antwerp.

'What's all this to-do?' shouted Master Kett.

She told him how Tom had vanished from the Fair. Kett groaned. 'Kidnapped, I'll be bound,' he said. 'Then we must find him very quickly, for they may not keep him alive. Or he could be taken to the coast and sold to a vessel as a ship's boy.'

He climbed back into the saddle. 'Ill go with the Watch,' he shouted. 'Send Alan and the other men after me.'

He galloped off in a cloud of dust and soon caught up with the Constable. 'Hurry!' he yelled. 'My son may already be lying in some ditch with his throat cut. Reward for the man that finds him, dead or alive.'

Chapter Four

The rattling and jolting of the cart woke Tom up. Every bone in his body hurt and the sack that covered his head was wet. Rain was falling on his bare feet. He tried to shout but the dirty rags were still tied round his mouth. Saltimbanco's donkey-cart was carrying him further and further away from the town.

It was a long time before the cart stopped. 'That's far enough, Neddy,' he heard a voice say. Tom recognised the Great Saltimbanco's voice. 'We can go no further today. There is a village up the

road with more people to sell pills to.' He
laughed to himself. 'But no more today.
Now it is sleep time. Just let me get your
feed-bag from the cart and then ... '

All of a sudden Tom felt the man's
hands on his legs. 'What?' the man
shouted. 'What's this? How did you ... ?'

The sack was pulled off Tom's head
and the gag untied from his mouth. 'Who
are you?' said Saltimbanco. 'And how did
you get here?'

Tom blinked the dust from his eyes.
'I am hurt,' he said. 'Fetch help and I will
reward you. Some men stole all my
clothes.'

Saltimbanco reached down to untie
him, but then stopped, 'Wait a bit,' he
said. 'If I fetch help, they will start asking
questions. They might even say that I
took you. They will want to know what I
was doing in your town. They might even
find out how I ... ' He rubbed his chin
and stood there.

Then Tom said something very stupid.
'They might find out how you magic eggs
out of thin air?' he said. 'I know that. I
was going to tell the crowd when the

beggars grabbed me.'

Saltimbanco narrowed his eyes. 'So,' he said, looking down at the boy. 'So you know about the eggs. That settles it. I cannot take you back.'

'Untie me, please,' said Tom. 'I promise I will not tell. Just untie me.'

But Saltimbanco was back on the front of the cart. 'Giddup, Neddy,' he said. 'It's on to a boat and over the sea for you and me until the trouble has died down.'

'Please!' Tom shouted. 'Let me go.'

The man turned round and lashed out with a short whip, catching Tom across his bare legs. 'Shut up!' he yelled. 'I have a mind to throw you into the sea. But wait, there's a cottage over there. Let me think.'

The cart came to a stop and Tom felt Saltimbanco get down again. The sides of the cart stopped him from seeing, but he heard voices. 'It's a mad boy,' he heard Saltimbanco say. 'He thinks he is from a rich family, but really he has run away from the madhouse. Just keep him for a night, to give me time to get to the coast. I will give you three pence if you do that.'

A woman's face came over the side of the cart and stared down at Tom. Her hair was straggly and she looked tired. 'Three pence is not enough. I want at least six pence,' she said. 'And what shall I do with him tomorrow?'

'Just turn him loose. By that time I will be safe and if anyone asks, say that you found him in the woods. He is mad, so they will just lock him up again.'

'No!' Tom shouted. 'Please. I am not mad. I am the son of a magistrate. You will be rewarded if you take me home.'

The woman's face came again. She looked at Tom's ragged shirt and torn hose. She saw the blood on his head and face. 'He has no shoes,' she said. 'And he is clearly very mad. The son of a magistrate would never look like that. Leave him with us. Give me the sixpence.'

Saltimbanco lifted Tom and carried him into a small house, stooping as he went under the low doorway. Inside it was dark and there was a smell of smoke and unwashed bodies. Tom was thrown into a corner onto a heap of straw. 'He can stay there till tomorrow,' said the woman. 'My husband will be home from the sheep soon. He will know what to do. Perhaps we will get a reward from the madhouse.'

Tom felt utterly miserable. There he was, miles from anywhere, still tied so that he could not move. And tomorrow he was to be taken to the madhouse. He burst into tears.

Then he felt a gentle touch on his arm. An older girl was kneeling by his side with a pan of water. 'Here, mad boy,' she said. 'Take a drink. It is good water from our well. See, I will wash the blood from your face.'

Cool water ran into his mouth and he felt a damp rag pass over his forehead. 'Thank you,' he said. 'You will be well rewarded when my father hears of your kindness.'

'Poor mad boy,' said the girl. 'Sleep now. No more talk. I will untie your hands and feet.'

Tom lay back on the straw. Now that he was free he thought of running, but all his bones hurt and his head was racked with pain. He closed his eyes against the smoke from the fire. Somebody threw a blanket over his bare legs. He slept.

Chapter Five

Tom woke up. Inside the cottage it was still dark. Somebody was rattling pans near the smoky fire. A chill wind gusted through the open door of the cottage.

He tried to sit up, but every part of his body hurt. He groaned and lay back again. He was on a heap of straw, still in his ragged shirt and hose. Near him lay three small children, all asleep. A large black dog was snuffling round. Some hens were pecking round the doorway.

A man came over and looked down at him. He was short and heavily built. A sheepskin coat was held round his waist with rope and he wore rough cloth leggings. 'Are you awake, boy?' the man said. His voice was gruff.

Tom put his hands behind him and pushed himself up. 'Yes,' he said. 'And I want to go home. Find me a horse. Hurry up!'

The man laughed. 'Find you a horse? I could just as easily find one of those great elephants that snort water up their noses. You really are mad.' He turned. 'Jane, bring the boy some bread and a pan of water. We must feed him before I take him away.'

'Listen to me,' Tom shouted. 'I am not mad. I was taken from the Fair by a man. It was that beggar who sometimes has one leg and sometimes two. He and some others robbed me and beat me. The Great Saltimbanco was making magic eggs and they threw me into his cart. Then ... '

The man laughed. 'Man with one leg or two? Great Salty-whatsisname? Magic eggs? You really are mad. Jane, that water.'

Tom felt very frightened. 'I am Tom Kett,' he said. 'My father is a magistrate and merchant. Please take me home to him and you will be rewarded. I am not mad, I tell you.'

The man scowled. 'I've heard of Kett. He's no friend to the poor. But you're making it up. You're just a crazy boy.'

'He is my father, I tell you,' said Tom, desperately. 'He deals in fine woollen cloth. He is in Antwerp in the Low Countries, but if you take me home, when he returns he will reward you well.'

'Fine woollen cloth, eh?' said the man. 'This Kett is one of those rich townsmen who have taken the land off us poor country people.'

He squatted on the floor and stared at Tom. 'There was a time when we had woods for our pigs to run in. Families had a cow and two goats on the village common. We had strips of land to grow crops. The woods provided us with wood and turf for our fires. There were nuts to gather and fruit for our children.'

He wiped sweat from his face. 'Then men like Kett took all that from us, put

fences round the common, chopped down the trees and brought in sheep. Sheep! It means that I have to work for the rich, look after other men's sheep instead of having my own crops and animals.'

He stood up and tightened his rope belt. 'Look round you, mad boy. This poor cottage is all we have and I must spend my days and nights with the sheep in all weathers, making money for men like Kett. Curse him and all like him.'

He spat into the fire, making it hiss. Tom was frightened. He had never heard anybody say anything like that.

But he still had some spirit left in him. 'Don't curse my father!' he shouted. 'Or I'll see that you are flogged and whipped and ... '

The man grabbed him by the scruff of the neck. 'Get up,' he yelled. 'You're a liar. I don't believe you. Stay there while I get a rope to drag you to the madhouse. If you talk like that when you get there you will find out what whipping and flogging are like.'

The girl Jane came with a pan of water to Tom. She put her arm round his back while he drank. Then she gasped. 'Father,' she said. 'See what the boy has round his neck.'

It was the hagstone, still on its leather. 'See this stone,' she said. 'I have heard of such things. They are to keep witches away from houses. And look at this fine leather-work.'

'Let me see,' said her father.

'That's not all,' said the girl. 'Look, on the stone, there is the sign of the cross. And see those other scratches. Letters.'

'Letters?' said her father. 'Tell me about them. I cannot read letters.'

The girl said, 'They are the letters H. K.'

'Henry Kett,' said Tom. 'My father's name.'

The man's face went pale. 'Perhaps he is telling the truth,' he said. 'If so, I am in bad trouble. If I take him home, he will tell his father what I said and I will be hanged. Best thing to do is to slit his throat and say that we have not seen him.'

The girl smiled. 'You know that you would not do that,' she said. 'You may be angry about the old way of life, but you would never kill anybody. No, let me take him home. He will not say bad things about us, will you, boy?'

Tom was crying. He said, 'No. Thank you. I think I can walk, but it will be a slow journey.' He struggled to his feet

The man gave him a hunk of brown bread. 'Go, young master,' he said. 'Forget you ever heard of us. Jane will see you to the edge of your town. Never come back here. Rich people have a way of dealing with men who say what I said. God be with you, and when you grow up, try to be a kind master to those who serve you.'

They set off, the girl leading. The sun was up and the rain had stopped. They went through fields of sheep, waded through a stream and then took a path into a dark wood. It went on for miles and after a while Tom needed to rest.

They sat under an oak tree. 'Tell me about your life,' Jane said. Tom told her about the house, the servants, his clothes, the food they ate.

'And do you go to school?' she asked. 'I wish I could go. I can read a little because the village parson showed me the letters on a horn book. And I can count up to a hundred so that I can help my father tell that all the sheep are safe.'

'If he has a hundred sheep, he must be rich,' said Tom.

Jane laughed. 'They are not his sheep. He is just the shepherd, spending his days and nights to make his master rich. But that's enough of that. Time we were on our way.'

'It's been a long walk, said Tom. 'We could do with that trickster's donkey cart.'

'The magic man?' said Jane.

'No magic. He has a wooden staff, hollow at one end. He puts raw eggs in the hole, then seals it up with fat. Then when he stirs the hot pan the fat melts. The eggs run out and - Hey Presto! Food from nowhere!'

'Amazing!' said Jane, her eyes wide open. 'What a bad man.'

'Bad for the folk he was cheating,' said Tom. 'And he was selling them pills that I am sure were ...'

He stopped because the trees had ended and they were out in the open again. 'It's not far now,' Jane said. 'The main track to your town goes past that old cottage with the broken roof. After about an hour's walk you will see the tower on your church. Now I must leave you.'

She turned, but Tom caught her sleeve. 'Wait,' he said. 'I can hear men's voices.'

They looked over at the old cottage and saw a small, bent man come out of the doorway. He was eating something. Tom gasped and his heart started to thud. 'We are lost!' he said. 'That man. Look. Do you see that blue velvet doublet?'

Jane said, 'Fine clothes for such as him.'

'It is one of the beggars who took me,' gasped Tom. 'Titch, they call him. That is my hat and my doublet.'

In his excitement he was almost shouting. Titch turned to look their way. Jane said, 'Stupid boy! He's seen us. We must run and hide.'

They stood up and dashed back into the trees, just as Stumper and some other men came out of the hut. Titch was pointing towards the wood. Tom saw that

Stumper was drawing a long knife from his belt. 'Run for your life,' he gasped. 'Or we shall be dead.'

Chapter Six

From behind them they heard a shout:
'It's that boy!'

'Get off the path,' Jane gasped. 'Now.'

They turned into the trees. Nettles
and brambles and small bushes slowed
them down. Tom went in front, but then
he heard Jane give a cry. She collapsed on
the ground. 'My leg,' she said with a
groan. 'I've twisted my knee.'

Tom gave her a hand, but she could
hardly walk. 'No use,' she gasped. 'You
run on. It's you they want. Leave me.
They won't hurt me.'

They had reached a small clearing and were standing under an old crab-apple tree. Tom said, 'Let's climb up there.' He pointed to a place in the lower branches of the tree. There the leaves were thick and they would be hidden from the ground.

Jane looked up and shook her head. 'I can't climb. My knee is giving way.' She looked up again. 'And in any case look, there's a huge wild bees' nest up there. We should be stung to death.'

They turned away from the tree, but to their horror, there in front of them, stood Stumper. He grinned, showing his black stumps of teeth. 'Got you, my beauties,' he grunted. 'Titch, Matt, come and get these two. What were you doing, eh? Spying? Going to turn us in to the Watch, were you?'

There was no escape. He came towards them with. 'Say your prayers, insects,' he hissed. 'No more spying for you two.'

But then suddenly everything changed. From behind them Tom heard the sound of men's voices and the barking of dogs. It was now the beggars' turn to run, but they were too late. A large group of armed men ran into the clearing. Tom's father and Alan were with them. It was the Watch.

'Father!' he yelled, but at the same moment Stumper caught hold of Jane and put his knife to her throat.

'Stay there!' he shouted. 'Or this girl dies. Stand back and let us go.' He held Jane in front of him and moved until his back was against the crab-apple tree.

'Let the girl go first,' said Master Kett.

Stumper shook his head. 'No. We go first or she dies now.' He touched Jane's neck with the knife and a spot of blood ran down her dress.

Tom had run to his father's side. How could he save Jane? If the beggars took her they would be sure to kill her. Her neck was bleeding.

He put his hand up to his own neck and felt the hagstone still hanging there. An idea came to him. Now was the time for the stone to fight evil. He took it off and held the leather band in his hand.

There was no time to waste. Tom swung the stone round his head, aimed

at the crab-apple tree and let go. The
hagstone flew like an arrow and hit its
target with a crash. It was the wild bees'
nest.

In a shower of dust the flimsy shell of
the nest collapsed. Out poured thousands
of wild bees, humming angrily.

There was panic as the bees attacked. Stumper dropped the knife and clawed at his face. The bees were like a dark mask all over it. Tom was stung too, but he ran across, grabbed Jane's hand and dragged her to safety. The Constable and some of the Watch had run away, but those that were left grabbed the beggars and dis-armed them. Then they all made for the open air.

Outside the wood they stopped. Most of the men were cursing and pulling bees out of their clothes. But there was something really odd. Most of the Watch had been badly stung, but the beggars were stung worse than anybody. Their hands and faces were covered with stings. Titch's eyes were closed with stings. Matt's mouth was blue and his lips were twice their normal size. Stumper's arms were worst of all, smothered in bumps and swellings.

Then the Constable came back, riding his horse. 'Well done, men,' he said.

Master Kett scowled at him. 'It was my boy that saved the day,' he said. 'He took a risk though.' He turned to Tom.

'It was lucky the bees went for the beggars first or things might not have turned out so well.'

Tom said, 'That was not luck. When Jane and I first saw the men coming out of the cottage, they were all eating bread. Something was dripping from the bread. Then, later on, when Stumper pulled his knife I saw that he had got sticky honey on his hands and in his beard. I guessed that they had robbed the bees of their honey and the bees might like to get their revenge.'

Stumper had been listening. 'Curse you and all insects like you,' he snarled. 'And curse all bees. I shall never eat honey again.'

Henry Kett roared, 'You certainly won't! You're going to the Lock-Up. All you get there will be bread and water. And then you'll be taken away and hanged from the gallows. See to them, Constable.'

When they had gone, Tom hugged his father. Then he looked round for Jane. But she had gone, slipped away after Tom had rescued her. Tom called her name, but there was no reply.

Master Kett listened while his son told him what had happened. When he heard about Jane's family, he nodded. 'It is true,' he said. 'Good men lost their living when the sheep came. But that was many years ago, before I was born. The man still has a cottage and he gets a daily wage of something like four pence.'

'That means that they really are very poor,' Tom said. 'And Jane was kind, even when she thought I was just a poor, mad boy.'

'You've changed,' said his father. 'Are you the same boy that wanted servants to do all the work? Are you the boy who was too important to help in the house, the boy who said the poor were just lazy?'

Tom said, 'That's true. I have learned something. But, please, Father, would you give Jane's family some money or do something to make their life better. They have nothing.'

He bent down and shook a few bees off the hagstone, which lay in the grass under the crab-apple tree. 'The hagstone saved the day,' he smiled. 'I'll hang it up again outside our house.'

He climbed up behind his father on the horse and they set off for home. Then after a while, he said, 'Father, if the Fair is still there, can I go?'